CHOOSE YOUR OWN ADVENTURE®

Kids Love
Choose Your O...

"I like the way you c... ... ...e way
the story goes."
Beckett Kahn, age 7

"If you don't read this book, you'll get payback."
Amy Cook, age 8½

"I thought this book was funny.
I think younger and older kids will like it."
Tessa Jernigan, age 6½

"This is fun reading. Once you go in to have an
adventure, you may never come out."
Jude Fidel, age 7

Illustrated by Keith Newton
Book design by Stacey Boyd, Big Eyedea Visual Design
For information regarding permission, write to:

CHOOSECO

P.O. Box 46
Waitsfield, Vermont 05673
www.cyoa.com

A DRAGONLARK BOOK

ISBN-10: 1-937133-43-5
EAN: 978-1-937133-43-6

Published simultaneously in the United States and Canada

Printed in China

0 9 8 7 6 5 4 3 2 1

OWN ADVENTURE®

SPACE PUP

BY R. A. MONTGOMERY

A DRAGONLARK BOOK

For Shannon

READ THIS FIRST!!!

WATCH OUT!
THIS BOOK IS DIFFERENT
from every book you've ever read.

Do not read this book from the first page
through to the last page.
Instead, start on page 1 and read until you
come to your first choice. Then turn to the
page shown and see what happens.

When you come to the end of a story,
you can go back and start again.
Every choice leads to a new adventure.

Good luck!

"Honey!" your mom calls from the kitchen.

You are with Homer, your dog, and Zogg, your cat, enjoying the first day of summer vacation.

"I'm here, Mom! With Homer and Zogg," you reply.

"I've got news for you," your mom says, walking over to the three of you.

"What, Mom?"

"Your friend Janice has invited you to Paris for a two-week visit!"

Turn to the next page.

"Me and Zogg and Homer can go to Paris?!" you shout, throwing your fist in the air.

"Well," says your mom, "I was thinking just you. It's hard for animals to travel on planes. And I think you need to spend a little bit more time with people, not just with animals!"

"They're more than just animals," you say. This isn't the first time that you have had this conversation. She just doesn't get it. Adults rarely do.

"You need the companionship of humans. Your pets can't talk, read, write, or do math." Your mom can be bossy.

"You would be surprised," you mutter under your breath.

"What was that?" she asks. She doesn't like to be contradicted.

"Oh, nothing, Mom, nothing."

Homer cocks his head and gives you a kind look. Zogg, the black-and-tan Maine coon cat, swishes her tail.

Turn to the next page.

"Should we visit Janice in Paris?" you ask Homer and Zogg.

Janice is your friend from school. Eduardo, you, and Janice are really good friends. Right now Eduardo is in Mexico City visiting his dad. His parents are divorced. Before Janice left for Paris, you, Homer, Zogg, and Janice called Eduardo with video chat every day to stay in touch. Eduardo and Janice like Homer and Zogg almost as much as you do.

You have a huge secret, a really big secret. Not even Janice and Eduardo know.

Turn the page if you want to find out the secret!

Homer and Zogg can speak English! At least when they are talking to you.

Other humans just hear woofs, yelps, screeches, purrs, and cries. You hear words. The three of you have long, good talks about lots of things, things that matter, like friendship, kindness, and growing up. Lots of stuff.

"France is far away," says Zogg. "And I don't think your mom will let us go with you. But it might be really fun for you! It's your choice."

"So, what are you going to do, buckaroo?" Homer asks. He sounds worried. The three of you had great summer adventures planned.

"If you guys can't come along, I don't want to go!" you tell them.

Homer stretches, scratches his side, and says: "Zogg and I had a plan for this summer too. We've been working on something top secret."

You raise your eyebrows at Homer.

Go on to the next page.

"When you see Zogg and me taking long naps we really aren't. We are getting transmissions from the Intergalactic Education Center."

"What's that?" you ask. Homer knows a lot of stuff, but sometimes you think he might be making it up.

Zogg speaks up. "It's like online college, except it's for life-forms from all planets in all galaxies, like the Milky Way and all the millions of other galaxies in the universe. They take students of any species."

"Even me?" you ask.

Turn to page 9.

"Well, so far no other humans even know about it! But we were going to invite you to go with us, even travel in space." Zogg gives a big swish of her tail, grins at Homer, and bats him with her paw.

"So, off to visit Janice in Paris or off to a different planet in our galaxy?" Homer looks right at you with clear eyes. Zogg turns her back.

If you choose to visit another planet, turn to page 11.

If you choose to go to see Janice in Paris, turn to page 12.

"Space!" you tell your dog and cat. As soon as the words leave your mouth, your backyard fills with sparkling lights and a huge sound.

Kazooma!! Scrooch!!

"Where are we?" you ask, getting excited but worried at the same time. You, Homer, and Zogg have arrived on a different planet. Zogg and Homer are wearing crowns. You touch your head. You have a crown too!

"We have arrived on planet Ploxx, not far into the galaxy and not too different from planet Earth," says Homer.

"And here is my dearest friend from Ploxx," Homer continues. "Be nice to him, he's a Squark."

Turn to page 14.

"Paris, France!" you say. "But I can't go without you guys."

"Don't worry. We'll meet you there at the Eiffel Tower," Homer announces in his know-it-all way.

"How?" you ask.

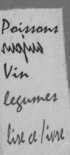

"Oh, we have our ways. Not to worry," Zogg replies before Homer gets a chance. She is a very smart cat.

Your dad arranges an airline ticket for you, takes you to the airport, and several hours later, you are in Paris. Janice isn't at her cousin's apartment. You decide to head for the Eiffel Tower.

Poissons

wopw

Vin

legumes

lire et livre

Turn to page 19.

14

You take one look at the Squark and want to run away.

Its hair is a bunch of vegetables: asparagus, celery, and eggplant. The Squark's face looks like a big tomato. It has a row of shining eyes. Its body is a lump of rock. The Squark sees your worried face and starts to grumble and wave its vegetable hair at you in a scary way.

Homer holds up a paw and says, "Squark, stop! This human is my friend."

Homer turns to you. "We are on a small planet. Squarks are part vegetable, part animal, and part mineral."

"How can that be?" you ask.

"Life takes many forms in the universe," says Zogg. "This is only one of millions of creature types. Be careful, though, I don't know if Squarks like humans."

"Why not?" you ask.

Turn to page 16.

Homer paws the ground. The Squark shakes his lumpy body. Zogg preens herself.

"Squarks take good care of this planet. They think Earth is a troubled planet," says Zogg.

"Troubled?" you say. "I know we have pollution, and it's a crowded planet, but…"

Homer speaks: "Squarks are afraid Earth will contaminate other worlds the way some insects attack plants."

"I'm just one human," you say, "but I would never attack this planet!"

"Tell the Squark!" says Zogg. "Maybe he'll believe you." Her crown sparkles.

Turn to page 23.

You like escapes. The Upside-downers are not evil, just not what you are used to. You think the mice could be nicer to the Upside-downers, but they are fun.

Whammo! Bongo! Socko!

Three rockets slam into the space around you, and tiny warriors surround you.

This is definitely not fun!

The warriors tie you up with silver ropes!

Is this The End? Could be.

Homer stands up, growls, and with a fierce look launches at the nearest bandit's leg.

"EEEyow!" the bandit yells. Homer goes after the next bandit, and then the next. The bandits don't wait for the boat to dock. They jump over the side and into the swirling water of the Seine. Fortunately, they have left the bags behind.

Turn to page 52.

Wow! The Eiffel Tower soars into the sky. You can hardly wait to go to the top. Homer and Zogg are waiting for you with tickets to go all the way up.

"Hey, you guys! Let's go. I want to see Paris from the top of this thing."

"The crowd is big, so just squish in," Homer says, squishing forward. You put Zogg in your backpack for safety. Away you go! You take the elevator to the tippity-top of the tower. What a view of all of Paris. It is beautiful. You wish Janice was here, but at least you are with Homer and Zogg.

"Hey, where is Homer?" Zogg screeches, her head poking out of the backpack. "He was just right beside you, and now he's gone."

Homer is missing. Homer is lost. "Not again!" you say, remembering the other times Homer has been lost.

Turn to page 20.

Homer is nowhere to be found.

"He must have been left behind," Zogg says. "Either that or he has been dognapped."

"Dognapped? Who would do a thing like that?" you ask.

Finally the elevator returns to the base of the tower.

"There he is!" Zogg says.

Sure enough, Homer is playing with a pretty French poodle! Her name turns out to be Rose. Homer speaks French, and they have quickly become new friends. Homer is found, but Janice still isn't home! What next? It's your summer vacation after all.

If you decide to stay in Paris, turn to page 38.

If you decide to change plans and go to Mexico and visit Eduardo, turn to page 46.

"What should I say? I want this…thing to know I am peaceful and won't hurt it!"

"I am not a thing!" the Squark says, anger rising in his vegetable voice. "You are!"

"Uh-oh, now you've done it," princely Homer says. "Run for it!"

"Where to?" you squeak.

"The puckerbrush," he replies. Princess Zogg has already disappeared.

The Squark moves remarkably fast for a creature with rocks for feet. "You will work for us for the rest of your life on our planet," the Squark says.

If you choose to turn and fight the Squark, turn to page 24.

If you dive into the puckerbrush, turn to page 34.

You take a firm fighting stance. You learned it in Tai Chi class at school. Your body is relaxed, and your center is calm and in control. You are ready to fend off any attack. Your moves will make your opponent slide by you. You will hurt no one.

The Squark stomps forward on its rock feet, tomato eyes flashing, turnip tops and radishes jiggling over its head.

Three more Squarks come to help him out! Two of them are lettuce-heads.

"Grab this Earthling. Take him to the factory!"

Off you go in the vegetable grip of two Squarks.

Turn to page 28.

"Homer! Zogg! Where are you?" you shout, heading for the puckerbrush.

It's right ahead. You ignore the thorns and dive in. Wow! You thought this was an ordinary bramble bush, but here on planet Ploxx it's not the same as on Earth. In between the prickles of the puckerbrush are a world of shining globes giving off many colors.

Turn to page 36.

"Hey, you guys, you always seem to get me in trouble. Why should I stay with you?"

"Trust us," Homer says. "Things are not always what they seem to be. Stay here, and you will learn things about the universe you won't believe."

"He's right," Zogg chips in, "the universe is amazing, and then we'll zip home faster than you could imagine on a thought beam."

"Okay, my friends," you reply, still wary of these two. "I'm in."

The trip to the outer reaches of the universe is like the night sky only much, much bigger with colors of the northern lights. Also, there is music that reminds you of rainbows at dawn on a summer morning after a rainstorm. You feel that you are a part of the universe, and it feels good.

"Time to go back home," Homer announces.

So, you grab a rainbow beam, and, thump, you are back home on the lawn outside your house.

The End

"What factory?" you shout.

"We make special food for deep-space crews on secret missions. Crews that travel beyond the limits of the universe."

"Let me go!" you plead.

The first Squark replies, "Don't worry, we won't eat you. We are vegetarians. You will work in the factory in the rhubarb section."

"Not rhubarb!" you shout. "I hate rhubarb!"

The Squarks ignore you and take you to a building made out of golden cubes.

"Three zorons for you! Work hard and maybe you will learn something on our planet. It will be a lesson you can take back to Earth with you so your planet is less sad."

"My planet is not sad," you reply, anger over-coming fear.

Turn to the next page.

"We could send you home, but it will take many zorons, much longer than the journey that brought you here."

"What's a zoron?"

"Six light years. But in Earth time it might just be seconds."

If you decide to try and escape and find Homer and Zogg, turn to page 26.

If you trust the Squarks, go home and turn to page 32.

"Deal. I go home and tell them about you and your perfect planet. I'm ready."

The Squarks go into a huddle, vegetable heads nodding in a gentle breeze.

You are beginning to get nervous again. What about Homer and Zogg?

"We must instruct you about growing healthy foods. We hear that you have developed poisons that spread to plant life. That you don't grow all the different types of plants and vegetables you could. This is very bad, we think."

"What do you want me to do back on Earth?" you say.

"Teach people—young people your age—that Earth is a sacred place, that it is your job to save it." All the Squarks nod their vegetable heads in agreement. "Are you ready?"

Go on to the next page.

If you are ready to return
to Earth, turn to page 40.

If you can't commit to this
mission, turn to page 72.

You don't make it to the puckerbrush. You are surrounded by four Squarks.

"This Earthling is causing trouble. What shall we do with this thing?"

"Let's send the Earthling on a mission to to deliver food to Deep Space. I know which spaceship we can send the Earthling on. It's called the Floosk 11."

"Great! Take the Earthling there, now!" the head Squark who looks like a giant tomato plant says. Then the Squark saunters away.

"Homer, Zogg, where are you when I need you?"

"We are here, you just can't see us. Have no fear," Zogg's voice says from somewhere. You wait, but you don't hear Homer's voice.

You are marched off to the transit zone airfield. It looks like a strawberry patch. You don't see any spaceship.

Go on to the next page.

One of the Squarks holds up a turnip and speaks into it. "Base to Floosk 11, ready to transfer food packages and their messenger. Contact. 10-4."

You don't see any food packages. A mouse walks up to you and the Squark.

Turn to page 50.

Prince Homer and Princess Zogg stand in a pool of golden light.

"Congratulations! You made it. Squarks aren't bad folks, just a bit pushy," says Zogg.

"Welcome back, Earthling! Welcome to the transit zone," says Homer, smiling a knowing smile.

"Transit zone? Where are we going now?" you ask, a bit worried. These travels are getting you into a lot of trouble.

Zogg smiles also. "You pick, of course!"

"How?" you ask.

"See this golden disc? It has symbols on it. Choose one, press it, and then get ready."

Turn to page 62.

"Let's stay in Paris," you suggest. "Janice isn't here, but maybe your new friend Rose can show us around," you say to Homer.

"Great! Okay with you, Rose?" Homer seems to really like Rose. *There is nothing worse than a lovesick dog*, you think. Except maybe a jealous cat. Zogg looks a little mad.

"My pleasure," says Rose. "We will start with a trip on the boat that goes up the Seine and shows wonderful views of my city. Follow me. The captain is my friend."

Turn to page 44.

You want to go back to Earth. Are all planets as weird as this one?

The universe is a strange and wonderful place. You remember that your science teacher showed a video that said that there are billions of galaxies! Billions. That's as many as all the grains of sand on a giant beach. It makes sense that there could be lots of different life-forms. Planet Earth has amazing kinds of beings: insects, fish, birds, and plants. Coral reefs are living animals. Creatures we have never seen live in the deep sea.

Time to go. Back to your home—good old planet Earth.

Off you go!

The End

Inside the base of the Observatory, you find yourself in a room of pictures. They are all of things that happened long ago. There is a colorful button below each picture.

You slowly move your finger to the button for the picture of a mountain covered with rain clouds. You press the button.

You begin to dissolve into this place. You see people. They are all farmers except for some angry leaders with beards.

"YOU! Yes, you! Come here," one of the angry leaders says to you, shouting.

"Push another button," Zogg suggests.

With a splash of golden light, you zoom into the future. It is a universe beyond comprehension. No wars. No poverty. No crime. You decide to stay for some time in this amazing world.

Turn to page 60.

The boat is a big tourist boat called a *Bateau Mouche*. You board it with a group of other tourists and take a seat on the top deck.

"Cast off!" the captain yells in French to the crew. The boat moves into the middle of the Seine. You cruise past Notre Dame, the famous cathedral, and past the Louvre, the great art museum. *What a view, what a city*, you think.

Suddenly there is a shout from the foredeck. "HELP!!! Bandits!"

Looking up, you see three men wearing sunglasses moving down the rows of seats forcing passengers to put wallets, money, watches, and jewelry in big shopping bags.

"Homer!" Rose screams. "You are so brave. Stop them!"

Turn to page 18.

You think about Mexico and you are almost instantly in Mexico. You can't believe it. Homer and Zogg are magical beings. But then, aren't we all magical beings?

You have another magical moment in the Yucatán: Eduardo steps out from behind a tangle of bushes.

"Welcome, my friends. Homer! Zogg! I'm so glad you came along. Now the adventure begins."

"Eduardo," you say, embracing him. Homer and Zogg smile in their own dog and cat way. "Where are we?" Behind you is a massive stone pyramid.

"We are in the Yucatán, and that is the pyramid of Chichén Itzá. It has a mysterious history. Not all good. Some terrible things happened here many hundreds of years ago. But it is also very powerful."

Turn to page 54.

The Yucatán and its mysterious pyramids, temples, and observatory lure you into this steamy jungle where jaguars hide, snakes slither, and people still live in ways that have existed for thousands of years. It is a land of enchantment. You decide that you want to be an archaeologist when you grow up. You want to discover who these people were, what they thought, and why their civilizations vanished. Or maybe you will discover they never vanished, they were just hidden from view?

"Sorry, Homer and Zogg, but I'm staying," you announce.

"That's fine with us," they reply. "We are at your service. Adventure is everywhere."

Turn to page 61.

"Ready?" the mouse squeaks. Underneath his mouse fur, his body is covered with diamonds.

"The transit flight is about to leave," the mouse pilot says.

A large, squiggly cylinder-shaped spacecraft pulls up. It must be the Floosk 11, you think. A hatch opens and out come three jewel-studded mice. They all give a mouse smile and a weird paw shake.

Turn to page 56.

Homer and Zogg are having a conversation in some strange language that you don't understand. When did they learn to speak this other language? Maybe they are aliens!

"On second thought," you say to Homer and Zogg, "just what is time travel?"

"Just like it sounds. Time past, time present, time future. You get to choose one of the three." Homer seems proud of himself. Zogg stares at you with her yellow eyes.

"Well, but, how?" you ask.

"Just follow us into the Observatory. You will see." Homer leads the way.

Turn to page 42.

"He is our hero!" people shout. Homer looks proud. Zogg hugs him and Rose leaps with joy. You are proud too. Homer is one great dog.

"Let's go to a bistro," Zogg says. "It's a French restaurant. We need to celebrate."

Off you go, the four of you, to a famous bistro called *Les Deux Magots*.

"That means two worms," Homer announces.

"No," says Zogg, "it is the name of two little statues inside."

They feed the four of you delicious food. Homer is the center of attention. Passengers from the boat give toasts to Homer and insist on buying your food.

What a day this has been. Where to next?

The End

The pyramid is amazing, but you feel a sense of gloom and doom also. You would rather explore the jungle or the waterfalls.

"Let's get out of here," you say. Zogg looks at you and nods her head. Homer is running around chasing a small iguana. Eduardo looks worried. He wants you to like his home.

Go on to the next page.

"Let's go see the Observatory," he suggests. "The ancient Mayans who built it knew a lot about mathematics and astronomy."

Homer woofs. He knows a lot about Mayans.

"They also wrote down stories about their beliefs and myths and made very good records of their trade. The Mayan civilization disappeared, and for a long time we did not know what the writing said. But now the codex has been broken, and we can read their language. We understand that this Observatory was built by wise people with a lot of knowledge. They worshiped what they saw from the building, and they thought about many of the mysteries that have fascinated all humans."

On to the Observatory!

Turn to page 66.

"All aboard for regions unknown!" the mouse pilot announces.

"Don't go!" Homer shouts. "You'll be sorry."

The problem is that so far Homer and Zogg have done nothing but get you in trouble. Should you listen to them, or should you ignore them?

If you take their advice, don't go on the Floosk 11 and turn to page 27.

If you go on the Floosk with the mice crew, turn to page 58.

"Goodbye," you say, waving to Homer and Zogg. You walk up the ramp into the space-ship. You almost don't fit—it's made for a mouse. Inside you find a straw nest for the mice and a control console made out of fur. Dials and screens cover the sides of the Floosk 11.

"All aboard, Captain," shouts a mouse lieutenant. "Let's squiggle off. Destination: Deep, Deep Space."

And so begins another strange journey into time and space.

Go on to the next page.

It doesn't take long to come to a bumping halt.

"What's that?" you ask, alarmed at the sudden stop.

"Oh, nothing. Maybe we hit a small planet or an asteroid or another space-ship. Happens all the time."

"What do we do?"

"Patience is a virtue, you Earthlings like to say. So be patient. The captain will fix everything."

The hatch opens and you are met by seven people standing on their heads. Two of them are walking backward on their hands!

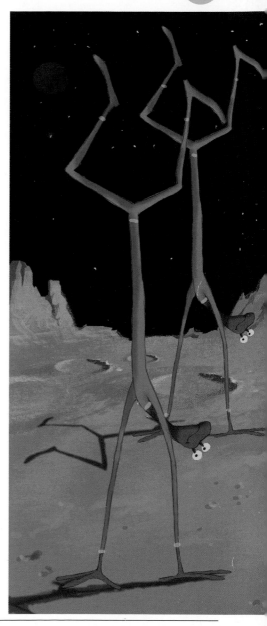

Turn to page 63.

The people or life-forms on these planets are such a wonderful collection of beings—so diverse, so incredible—that you travel from planet to planet in awe of life. It reminds you of the great science museum in Boston back in your own universe on planet Earth and of the aquarium in Baltimore and the Great Barrier Reef off Australia.

"Seen enough?" Homer asks. He seems proud of himself.

"Not yet," you reply. For a budding archaeologist, this is just the beginning of a life filled with wonder.

"Your choice, doctor," Zogg says, "but we have to go now. See you around!"

With a swoosh of tails, you are on your own in this universe of life!

The End

It is wonderful to have such good friends, you think. You hope you are as good a friend to them as they are to you.

You become a world-famous archaeologist specializing in Mayan culture. Of course Homer and Zogg have helped you all the way. They are more than just pets, as you well know. They are magical beings!

The End

You hesitate. Is this a wise move? But then you move your finger to the disk and touch the spiral.

Turn to page 65.

"Oh, NO! I hate this planet," the mouse captain says. "Upside-down things have smaller brains than space fleas!"

"Hate's not good," you say. "They are just as different as mice with jewels on their bodies instead of fur."

"Easy for you to say! I think they've tricked us. We shouldn't stop here."

If you escape with the Floosk team, turn to page 17.

If you decide to stay with the Upside-downers on this strange planet, turn to page 69.

"Good choice," purrs Zogg. "Good choice indeed. You have chosen to visit the world of the black holes. They are the most profound of all things in the universe." Zogg smiles.

"How do we get there?" you ask.

"Follow me," says Homer.

One step and you are in a narrow, silver beam of light. A swooshing sound surrounds you. You hurtle through space approaching a wormhole in time. It is the entrance to a black hole.

You tumble down a slippery chute into the black hole and come to a bumpy landing. Bright light surrounds you, and music plays. Homer and Zogg stand by a lake fed by three streams: time past, time present, time future.

"This is what the universe is all about," Zogg says. "Only endless time and space and experience. There is no end, there is no beginning."

"Will we be here forever?" you ask.

"We'll find out!" says Zogg.

The End

The Observatory is a platform you stand on to view the solar system. You feel the excitement of the place and the wonders of life.

"This is great!" you say.

"Do you want to see much, much more?" Homer asks, tugging at you.

"Like what?" you ask, already overwhelmed by what you are seeing.

"Like deep space, distant stars, other planets, and galaxies," Homer and Zogg say together.

"How?" you ask.

"Time travel. It's simple, fairly safe, and fascinating," answers Homer.

If you decide to stay where you are because there is more to see in this mysterious land of the Yucatán, turn to page 48.

If you decide to accept the time travel, turn to page 51.

"My space pup! Where are you? Astro cat, where are you?" you plead. Your decision to stay with the Upside-downers might not be the smartest one.

"We're here, boss. You worry too much," Homer says, adjusting his crown. Zogg is scratching her side with her right hind leg.

An Upside-downer approaches you. "I am Alfred. I think mice are pests. Good riddance!" Alfred takes your arm and pulls you in the direction of a giant upside-down castle, with its turrets sticking into the ground and its gates at the top.

Music blares from speakers, but it sounds like it too is backwards. Suddenly Alfred screams, "ATTACK!"

Turn to page 70.

"Attack? Who is attacking?" you shout. But the Upside-downers are gone, running away backward on three-fingered hands.

An armada of spacecraft approaches with rockets blasting the ground. Where can you hide?

POOF!!!!! You wake up in the hammock in your backyard. Homer and Zogg are curled up underneath you. Homer is snoring dog snores and Zogg snuffles and purrs.

The End

Homer and Zogg walk up to you as if everything is fine.

"All aboard for planet Earth!" Homer shouts.

With a whirling, spinning, tumbling dance, the three of you dance through time and space back to your house.

"Mom, what's for supper?" you yell.

The End

ABOUT THE AUTHOR

R. A. Montgomery has hiked in the Himalayas, climbed mountains in Europe, scuba-dived in Central America, and worked in Africa. He returns to France every winter, travels frequently to Asia, and calls Vermont home. Montgomery graduated from the Williston-Northampton School and Williams College and attended graduate school at Yale University and NYU. His interests include macro-economics, geo-politics, mythology,  history, mystery novels, and music. He wrote his first interactive book, *Journey Under the Sea*, in 1976 and published it under the series name *The Adventures of You*. A few years later Bantam bought this book and gave Montgomery a contract for five more, to inaugurate their new children's publishing division. Bantam renamed the series *Choose Your Own Adventure*. Today Montgomery continues to write and publish new *Choose Your Own Adventure* books. He is married to Shannon Gilligan.

ABOUT THE ILLUSTRATOR

Keith Newton began his art career in the theater as a set painter. Having talent and a strong desire to paint portraits, he moved to New York and studied fine art at the Art Students League. Keith has won numerous awards in art such as The Grumbacher Gold Medallion and Salmagundi Award for Pastel. He soon began illustrating and was hired by Walt Disney Feature Animation where he worked on such films as *Pocahontas* and *Mulan* as a background artist. Keith also designed color models for sculptures at Disney's Animal Kingdom and has animated commercials for Euro Disney. Today, Keith Newton freelances from his home and teaches entertainment illustration at the College for Creative Studies in Detroit. He is married and has two daughters.

For games, activities, and other fun stuff, or to write to R. A. Montgomery, visit us online at CYOA.com